Searching for Skye

An Arctic Tern Adventure

written and illustrated by Gail Clarke

This book is for Lily, Phoebe, Frank, Digby, Mali and Samson

and, of course, for....................................... (your name)

On the Arctic shore on a clear spring day
Two small speckled eggs in a stony nest lay.
Mum and Dad tern kept them warm day and night
Watching in case there was danger in sight.

And at last a sound like a tap or a scratch
Told them their babies were ready to hatch.

The newly hatched chicks were fluffy and small;
They didn't have any real feathers at all.
They sat in the nest with their beaks open wide
So their parents could pop something tasty inside.
And those two baby terns ate and slept all day long
Until they had grown both healthy and strong.

The parent terns thought that their young ones were clever;
The smartest and best-looking baby terns ever.
Mum decided to call them Pilot and Skye.
"Great names," agreed Dad, "when they know how to fly!"

And in a few weeks the baby terns grew,
Their fluffiness went and grey feathers came through.
A black feather cap appeared on each head,
"You are growing up fast!" their proud mother said.
"Tomorrow we'll start to teach you to fly,"
Father tern added to Pilot and Skye.

They began the next day. Dad called, "Just follow me,
And flap your wings hard while I count up to three."
Mum held her breath, not a word did she say
As her young ones took off in a wobbly way.

She peeked through her wing as they circled around
And smiled as they both came back safely to ground.
"Fantastic!" she cried. Father agreed,
"A little more practice is all that you need."

Their flying improved and in just a few days
They could catch their own food in a number of ways:
Diving into the sea to spear fishes to eat,
And capturing insects in flight for a treat.

"I think that we're ready," Dad said one fine day,
"In a very short time we must be on our way."
"On our way where?" Pilot asked quite excited.
"Can we come too? Have we both been invited?"

"Everyone's going, young and old too,"
Replied father tern, "it's what we terns do.
Before winter comes we start our migration,
Antarctica's shore is our next destination.
From North Pole to South Pole we follow the sun
Halfway round the world to where summer's begun."

The tern babies listened with eyes open wide
And when Dad had finished they cheerfully cried,
"How long will it take and when do we start?"
"Can we leave now? We can't wait to depart!"

"Slow down!" said Mum smiling. "We first have to make
A plan and decide on which route to take.
Your father and I are meeting tonight
With a large group of terns who will join in our flight.
You two stay here and be good little chicks;
Don't go out on your own and no silly tricks!"

The parents flew off. Skye waited a while
Then her face lit up with a mischievous smile.
She stretched out her wings, rose into the air,
Calling out to her brother, "Come if you dare!"

"Come back!" Pilot cried. "We promised to wait."
But Skye didn't hear him - his words were too late.
"I'll be back very soon," she called in delight,
And flapping her wings she flew out of sight.

Pilot sat in the nest as he waited for Skye
But she didn't come back and the hours drifted by.
He started to worry – he knew there were dangers –
Mum and Dad weren't around to protect them from strangers.
Then at last the beating of wings made it clear
To the worried young tern that his parents were near.

They landed and Pilot told them the tale.
Mum started to cry and Dad looked quite pale.
"We must search for our baby, there's no time to rest
Till Skye is back with us and safe in the nest."

They searched through the night and all the next day
But where Skye had gone to, no one could say.
They circled the skies, they asked all around,
But wherever they looked she couldn't be found.
The parents were sad – it was as they had feared:
Their adventurous baby had just disappeared.

After several more days father tern shook his head,
"A decision like this is not easy," he said.
"We have to consider the other terns too,
And thousands of birds cannot wait for a few."

"But what about Skye?" Pilot cried in dismay,
"We can't leave her here; she won't find the way."
The tears filled his eyes and ran down his beak
As Mum looked on sadly, unable to speak.

"Perhaps," Dad continued," Skye has been found
By a flock that's already Antarctica bound.
And if she's gone with them there might be a way
For our family to be reunited one day.
We must keep up our spirits and hope for the best,
Letting luck and good fortune take care of the rest."

Summer came to an end; the terns knew they must go
Before the arrival of ice, sleet and snow.
The long journey south would take ninety days –
There was no time to waste on further delays.
They were ready to go; they had made preparations;
It was time for the longest of all bird migrations.

Leaving the Arctic Circle they'd fly
For hundreds of miles day and night through the sky.
Till hungry, exhausted and ready to drop,
They'd reach the Antarctic – and there they would stop.
And for three summer months the terns would remain
Before heading back to the Arctic again.

Terns make this marathon journey each year,
So throughout their lives it will soon become clear
They fly thousands of miles. How many? Don't swoon!
More than three times the distance from Earth to the Moon!
Seeing more daylight hours from the time of their birth
Than all other creatures that live on the Earth.

The day for departure had finally come;
The cold air was filled with a low whirring hum.
As beating their wings they rose into the sky
And the terns waved the Arctic a cheerful goodbye.

"Stay close to us, Pilot," were Dad's kindly words,
"We'll protect you from dangers and unfriendly birds.
Don't stray from the group; stay well within sight
On your very first marathon pole-to-pole flight."
"I will," Pilot answered, his voice not quite steady,
Whispering softly, "I hope that I'm ready!"

The mid North Atlantic was where they were going
And thanks to the helpful winds that were blowing
They completed this stage of their journey quite fast
And could feed on fresh fish and plankton at last.
Once rested and fed, they flew on past the shores
Of a small group of islands called The Azores.

The dangers were many; the journey was long;
The icy-cold winds were frightening and strong.
And once in the evening a cry, loud and clear,
Warned all the terns that danger was near.

"What's happening?" cried Pilot, filled with alarm.
"Don't worry," Dad said, "you will come to no harm.
Some large gulls are near - they may try to attack –
There are only a few and we terns can fight back."

And as Pilot watched with eyes open wide
He stopped feeling scared and his heart filled with pride
As Dad and the other terns made it quite clear
To the fierce group of gulls that they weren't welcome here.
The terns were much smaller but thanks to their skills
They frightened the gulls with their sharp, pointed bills.
With a beating of wings the gulls flew away;
The terns all cheered loudly and shouted, "Hooray!"

Cape Verde Islands

Africa

Which Way?

South America

Brazil

Continuing south for many more miles,
They finally came to the Cape Verde Isles
Where each Arctic tern had a hard choice to make:
Which of the two different routes should they take?

Half of the group would continue to fly
Down the African coast, while the others would try
To cross the Atlantic and fly further still,
As they followed the eastern coast of Brazil.

Till all of the terns joined together once more
Coming safely to land on Antarctica's shore.
On the Weddell Sea ice-packs they happily found
A safe summer home and a good hunting ground.

Weddell Sea

Antarctica

"Pilot, we've made it!" Mum and Dad gasped,
As the huge group of terns landed safely at last.
"Our marathon flight is now over and done,
You are such a brave tern; we're proud of you, son."
But no answer came, not even a peep:
Pilot, exhausted, had fallen asleep.

It was now time to rest and on cold starry nights
The terns told each other of long-distance flights;
Of adventures they'd had; of dangers they'd seen;
Of routes they had chosen; of places they'd been.

Then Pilot's mum, with a tear in her eye,
Told them the story of how they'd lost Skye.
All of the terns, young and old too,
Said how sorry they were – it was all they could do.

But this isn't quite where our tern story ends.
Several days later one of their friends
Came to see Mum and Dad because he had heard
An incredible tale of a young baby bird.
Lost and alone, one night she'd been found
By a kind pair of terns when she fell to the ground.

She was tired, she was hungry, the pair did their best
To give her good food and plenty of rest.
Then finally when she was healthy and strong,
They flew from the Arctic and took her along.

Could this be Skye who'd been lost months ago
Before leaving the Arctic? It just might be so.

Now his parents thought Pilot was safely in bed,
But he'd heard every word their new friend had said.
"We've got to go now!" he excitedly cried,
Flapping about, his eyes open wide.

Their friend added cheerily,
"I'll lead the way.
It won't take us long,
I am happy to say."

And as he had promised they landed quite soon,
Finding their way by the light of the moon.
A small group of terns was standing around
Anxiously waiting for them on the ground.
And there in the middle as plain as could be
Was the happiest sight they ever could see.

"Skye," whispered Mum in a voice soft and clear,
As Skye flew to her side and the crowd gave a cheer.
Crying and laughing they all hugged each other;
Brother and sister, father and mother.
Their friends old and new, all were delighted:
The family of terns was at last reunited.

Arctic Tern Points

Adult Arctic terns have:

[ ] red beaks and fluffy head   [ ] blue caps and black feet
[ ] black feather caps and red or orange beaks

Adult Arctic terns are:

[ ] white with a black cap, red feet and grey wings   [ ] grey with blue caps and black feet
[ ] blue caps and black feet

Arctic terns build their nests:

[ ] in tall trees   [ ] on the Arctic shore
[ ] underground in caves

The nests are mostly made of:

[ ] stones and pebbles   [ ] grass and feathers
[ ] anything they can find

The eggs are kept warm by:

[ ] mum   [ ] dad
[ ] both parents

Young terns can fly:

[ ] as soon as they are born   [ ] after a few weeks
[ ] after a year

When Arctic terns are migrating they:

[ ] do not eat at all   [ ] eat when they land every night
[ ] catch insects on the wing and dive for fish

When the baby terns hatch out of the eggs they are:

[ ] featherless   [ ] just like their parents
[ ] grey or brown and fluffy

If Arctic terns attacked by their enemies they:

[ ] fly away at once   [ ] dive into the sea to hide
[ ] fight them off with their sharp, pointed bills

Migrating Arctic terns travel:

[ ] as far as from England to America each year   [ ] round the world each year
[ ] it depends if they want to migrate or not

Migrating Arctic terns fly:

[ ] through the day and stop every night   [ ] only at night
[ ] all day and night and hardly ever stop

Migration takes about:

[ ] 90 days   [ ] one week
[ ] one year

Arctic terns stop at a group of islands called:

[ ] Hawaii   [ ] The Azores
[ ] The Seychelles

After they reach the Cape Verde Islands:

[ ] they all fly down the coast of South America   [ ] they all fly down the coast of Africa
[ ] some take one route and some take the other

Arctic terns spend the European winter:

[ ] somewhere warm and sunny   [ ] at the North Pole
[ ] on the edge of the pack ice at the Weddell Sea

A note from the author

Dear Readers,

When I was writing this story I discovered many interesting facts about animals and migration.

One of the most amazing is how far some animals travel. From reading this book you now know that Arctic terns fly incredible distances during their lifetimes. What other animals do you know of that migrate thousands of kilometres?

Can you find out about other migrating animals? I would really enjoy hearing about them. Perhaps I could write another story!

If you want to ask me any questions about this story or tell me something interesting about migrating animals, I would love to hear from you.

gail@gailclarkeauthor.com   www.gailclarkeauthor.com

Other books by Gail Clarke

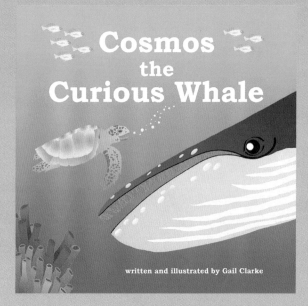

Printed in Great Britain
by Amazon.co.uk, Ltd.,
Marston Gate.